THE [illegible]

#1

Smarty Pants!

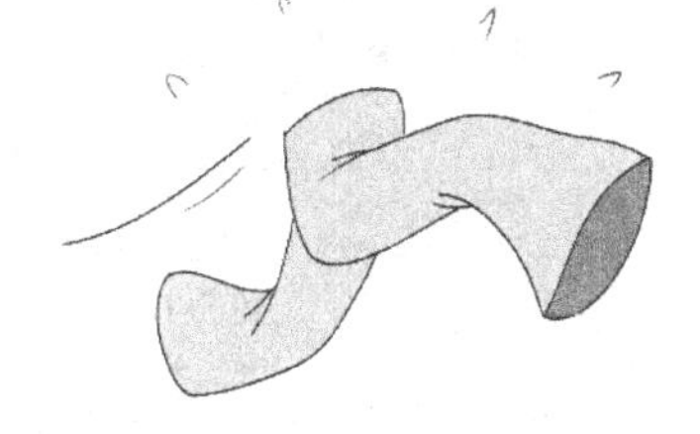

Brian Rock

Illustrated by Joshua Dawson

This book is dedicated to everyone who ever thought their day couldn't get any worse – and was wrong!

Published by First Light Publishing
Richmond, VA

Library of Congress Control Number: 2017908478
Rock, Brian. The Tyler Files #1 Smarty Pants
Dawson, Joshua. Illustrator

Summary: When Tyler's pants mysteriously come to life, he must find a way to make it through the day without becoming the school laughingstock. More importantly, he must survive his pants' "off the cuff" remarks to the school bully (and to his secret crush!)

ISBN# 978-0-9754411-3-8

1. School–Fiction. 2. Fantasy--Fiction. 3. Humorous stories 4. Mystery

Chapters

Bonus Material!

1

A Pair of Smarty Pants

My name is Tyler and I have a big problem.

My pants won't stop talking to me!

I know it sounds crazy, but it's true.

Yesterday I was a perfectly normal kid: I had a normal daydream in English class. I made some normal spitballs with my buddy Paul. I had normal conversations with my (mostly) normal friends.

But today I'm trying to avoid all those normal people so they don't see me having conversations with my own pants!

It all started this morning in Science class…

I had finished my photosynthesis assignment early. So I asked Mr. Beaker if Paul and I could use the last few minutes of class to study for a math test that we had in last period.

Mr. Beaker ran his thumb and forefinger along his goatee for a moment as if he was in deep thought. Then he said, "I'll tell you what, Tyler. If you can answer a question on photosynthesis, I'll let you and Paul take the rest of class to study math."

"Don't do it!" whispered Paul. "He's trying to trick you into learning something."

"OK," I said confidently. "What's your question?"

"What is the name of the green pigment in plants that absorbs sunlight?" asked Mr. Beaker.

"Chlorophyll." I answered.

"Oh no," moaned Paul.

"That's right!" cheered Mr. Beaker. "You and Paul may study your math."

So Paul and I got our notebooks and started studying together.

Sarah walked by and whispered, "Study all you want. You still won't get as good a grade as me." Then she smiled and waved so everyone would think she just said something nice to us.

"That Sarah thinks she's such a smarty pants," I said to Paul.

Suddenly I heard a weird voice say, "Hey! I'm a smarty pants too!"

Paul's eyes got really big. He looked at me, then he looked around the room.

"Who said that?" he whispered.

Before I could answer, the voice spoke again.

"I said that. Look down here!"

Slowly, I bent down to look under my desk. I was half afraid of what I might find. At first I didn't see anything.

"Over here," said the voice. Then I looked closer and realized it was my pants! They were talking!

MY PANTS WERE TALKING!!!

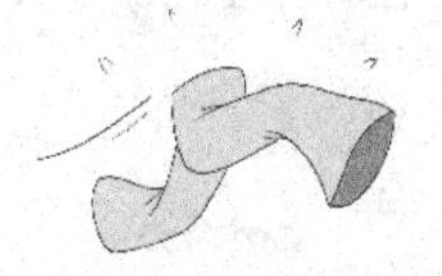

2

Get Serious

I wanted to scream and run out of the room, but that would've gotten me detention for sure. I squirmed in my seat, trying to figure out what to do. I looked around the room trying to see if anyone else had noticed. No one had. I looked at Paul for help. He shrugged his shoulders and turned his palms upward like he does in Math class when he doesn't know the answer to a question.

A thousand questions raced through my mind. Why were my pants talking? Why were my pants talking? Why were my pants talking?

OK, so I didn't have a thousand questions. But that one question went through my mind a thousand times.

Not knowing what else to do, I finally stammered, "H-H-How are you able to talk?"

"Like I said, I'm a smarty pants."

I watched as the denim fly of my jeans flapped up and down over my zipper as he spoke. It was creepy and fascinating at the same time. But what about the zipper? Was that its teeth? What would happen if it got hungry? What if…

"How can you be smart?" Paul interrupted my thoughts. "You're just a pair of pants."

"It's in my jeans," said the pants. "My mother was a lab coat and my father was a NASA parachute.

Don't believe me? Go ahead and ask me a tough question."

"OK," I said. "What's the value of X in 3X minus nine equals 12?"

"Seven," said my pants.

I checked my math book. He was right!

"That was too easy," said my pants. "Ask me a tough question."

"OK," said Paul. "How can I shoot spitballs at Sarah without getting in trouble?"

"Get serious Paul," I said, raising my voice.

"Shhhh!" scolded Mr. Beaker from the front of the class.

"Get serious," I whispered. "I can't walk around school all day with a pair of talking pants! What am I going to do?"

"You're looking at this all wrong," said Paul. "Instead of freaking out, you should be happy."

"Happy?"

"Yeah, happy," answered Paul. "Now you don't need to worry about that math test today. All you have to do is ask the questions out loud and have your pants give you the answers. Just make sure you guys are loud enough for me to hear."

"Excuse me!" said my pants. "First of all, it's very rude to talk about someone when they're right in front of you. And second, I will not help anyone *cheat* on a test."

"Whooa," said Paul. "Who said anything about cheating? I was just suggesting a little verbal encouragement."

"By the way," Paul continued, "It's really awkward talking to your pants. I don't know if I can keep doing this. People might think I'm weird."

"Come on Paul! Don't wig out on me. You *have* to help me! I can't have anyone else find out about this, or I'll be the laughingstock of the whole school."

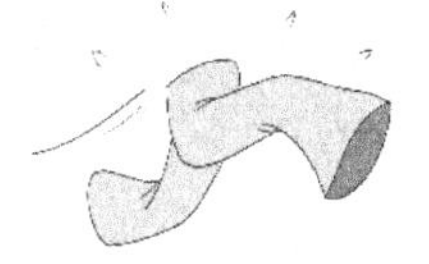

3

Indigestion

"What do you mean you can't help me?" I asked Paul over the sound of the class bell.

"I have to have lunch with Principal Stern today because of that spitball incident with Sarah last week."

"But what am I going to do? What if someone sees me talking to my pants? What if kids laugh at me?"

"Calm down, Tyler. I'll catch up with you in gym class. Just tell your pants to zip it until then."

So I walked to the cafeteria, hoping my pants would stay quiet. I'm not the kind of kid that likes a lot of attention. And I certainly didn't want the kind of attention that talking pants would bring! At least there was one bit of good news: we were having my favorite lunch today - spaghetti and meatballs! I was just about to get in line for a plate of spaghetti and a brownie for dessert when I felt my legs moving in a different direction.

My pants were controlling where my legs were walking!

“Where are you going?” I demanded, gritting my teeth like a deranged ventriloquist so no one would see me talking.

“What’s it to you, twerp!” said Rhino Rob. I was so busy watching what my pants were doing, I nearly ran into the biggest kid in school!

“Um, sorry.” I stammered as I quickly walked away.

"Where are you taking me?" I said to my pants, pretending to cough into my hand so other kids wouldn't think I was some kind of weirdo who talks to his pants.

"I'm taking you to get a nice cheese and apple plate for lunch," answered my pants.

"Why?"

"Two reasons," said my pants. First, you really should stick to natural fibers. Second, when you eat spaghetti, you eat too much and it starts to get a little crowded down here."

"Nevermind!" I grumbled. "Let's just get a seat."

After making me get a healthy choice plate, my pants seemed content to let me be in charge of walking again. I looked around and found an empty seat far away from everyone else. I didn't want anyone to hear what was going on - it's embarrassing when sounds come out of your pants!

So I sat alone. I took a bite of my apple, and watched everyone else enjoy their spaghetti. I tried to figure out how I could be alone all day without anyone else hearing my pants. I seriously considered trying to make myself sick or get in a fight so I would be sent home from school. But either way, kids would still laugh at me. And I might even get hurt. By the end of lunch, I was just grateful that my pants had gone a whole twenty minutes without mouthing off and getting me in trouble with someone else.

Maybe it was all just a weird daydream. Maybe I wasn't actually wearing crazy, talking pants after all.

Just then I saw Audrey, the really cute girl from Ms. Diphthong's homeroom. I've had a crush on her for a year, but she's never even noticed me. She was getting up from her lunch. She was headed right for my table!

My palms got sweaty. My heart beat faster. I looked away so she wouldn't think I was gawking at her. She was almost past me. I was about to exhale in relief, when my pants blurted out, "Whoa! Did it just get really hot in here?"

Audrey stopped. She turned back to look at me.

I was freaking out!

I felt a knot in my stomach the size of four apples. Audrey was looking right at me! I struggled to find something to say.

But suddenly Audrey's expression changed. She smiled. She smiled at me!

Not knowing what else to do, I waved and said, "Hey."

Before I could even get mad at myself for saying something so dumb; Audrey said, "Hey," then turned and walked out the cafeteria.

"She seemed nice," said my pants.

"What! You, ya…youuu…" I stammered, trying to control myself.

"You nearly made of fool of me in front of the cutest girl in school!" I said in my sternest possible whisper. "Plus, you almost got me beat up by the biggest kid in school. And the day's only half over! My resource class is next period, so I need you to be quiet. Do you understand me? Quiet! Quiet! Quiet!"

"Who you telling to be quiet, twerp!" yelled Rhino Rob, poking a finger in my chest.

How did I not see him coming?

"I was talking to myyyyy, uh… apple," I stammered. "It was begging me not to eat it, but I told him to be quiet or I'll bite him in half."

"That's your second strike," said Rhino. "One more and I'll bite you in half!"

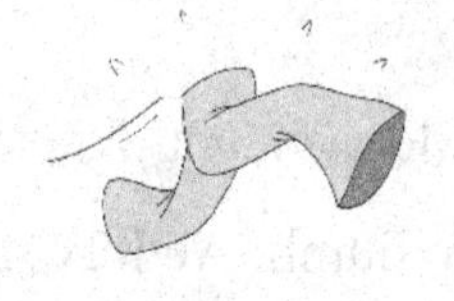

4

Shhhhh!

"Why is it so quiet in here?" blurted my pants.

"Shhhhhh!" scolded Mrs. Taciturn, the Librarian.

"Because it's the library," I whispered. "You're supposed to be quiet in here."

"Library!" said my pants. "Why didn't you say so? Let's go get a book!"

My pants got me up and started walking through the aisles of books.

"I don't have time for this!" I whispered. "I have to study for my math test."

"Fine," said my pants. "Just let me find a book to read while you study. Hey, this looks like a fun title: CHINOS, BREECHES, & TROUSERS, A HISTORY OF PANTS."

"Fine," I said. "I'll get your dumb book for you. But how are you going to read it?"

"Just set it on your lap. I'll read it with my button eye while you read your precious math book on the table."

"OK," I whispered. "But be quiet!"

I went back to my seat and opened the pants book. I set it on my lap while I opened my math notebook and tried to study.

Mrs. Taciturn gave me a curious glance.

I started reading the chapter on coefficients: 'a coefficient is a number placed before a variable…'

"This is interesting," interrupted my pants. "Did you know that ancient Mongolian horsemen first started wearing pants in the 6th century B.C.?"

"Shhh!" I said.

"SHHHHHH!" said Mrs. Taciturn, glaring at me.

"Sorry," I mouthed to her.

I went back to my math and tried to concentrate. Now where did I leave off? Variables? Or was it coefficients? It certainly wasn't very efficient.

"Holy Levis!" said my pants. "The name pants comes from an early saint – Saint Panteleon."

"Be quiet!" I whispered.

Mrs. Taciturn looked over the rim of her glasses at me.

"I can't help it," said my pants. "This book is so exciting! Did you know that pants were invented way before underwear? It says that underwear didn't come into common usage until the 1300's!"

"Waaaait a minute… Oh no!"

"What's wrong?" I asked.

"Don't you see?" asked my pants. "If pants were invented in the 6th century B.C. and underwear wasn't invented until the 1300's, then that means for almost two thousand years innocent pants had nothing to protect them from… from… from – naked human behinds! Ewwww!”

“Shhhhh!” said Mrs. Taciturn.

I looked back at her, held my hands out and shrugged to let her know it wasn’t me talking.

Suddenly, I felt my legs moving on their own. My pants were taking control again.

“I’ve got the heebie jeebies!” cried my pants. “I feel like I’ve got ants in my pants! I need to get up and move around!”

“No you don’t!”

“Yes I do!” said my pants as they swung my legs off the side of the chair and stood me up.

I fumbled to grab my math notebook as my pants tried to turn me around.

"I, um, need to go to the bathroom." I said to Mrs. Taciturn as my pants walked me out of the library. "I'll be right back – I hope!"

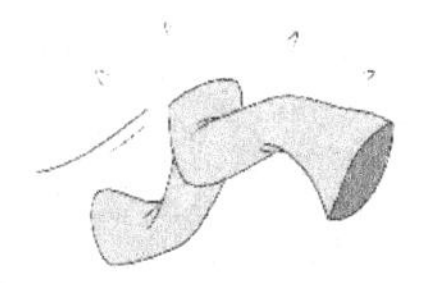

5

Boogie Fever

"I'm never going back there again!" sighed my pants. "I think I'm going to have nightmares for weeks!"

"It's your own fault, you know. If you would have helped me with my math, or at least STAYED QUIET like I asked, none of this would have happened."

"That's easy for you to say, you're not the one who had to endure naked behinds in your face for two thousand years! I think I just need to go for a walk and clear my thoughts."

"You can't just get up and walk around without a hall pass," I said. "You'll get me in trouble."

"You know for someone who wears relaxed fit pants, you're pretty uptight," said my pants. "Besides, it's not like we're going to burst into another classroom and break out in dance."

"I would hope not," I said.

"Wait, what's that sound?" asked my pants.

We were walking towards Ms. Treble's music class. She was playing "The Farmer in the Dell" for next week's recorder concert. All of us fifth graders had been practicing that song for the past month. By now I was absolutely sick of it. I hated even hearing the song.

"I love that song!" cheered my pants.

Suddenly my legs slowed and turned towards Ms. Treble's class.

"Oh no! You wouldn't!" I gasped.

Despite my best efforts to hold my legs still, my pants were moving my legs up and down in time with the music. I looked like a spastic frog as I struggled against my pants. They waltzed me right into Ms. Treble's class. I looked up to see the whole class staring at me! Even worse, this was Audrey's music class. She was staring at me too!

Ms. Treble hadn't seen me yet. She was going over to restart "The Farmer in the Dell" on the stereo. I wanted to run while I had the chance. But I stood, frozen in fear, for what seemed like hours in the deafening silence.

The song started again and my pants made me do the most embarrassing jig in the history of the world. I was so upset, I just crossed my arms and tried not to make eye contact with anyone.

"Tyler!" cried Ms. Treble. "What are you doing here?"

I looked up to see Ms. Treble walking toward me with her baton.

I wanted to leave, but my pants had other ideas.

The closer Ms. Treble got, the more I tried to back out the door. The more I tried to back out the door, the more my pants danced me back into class. For the rest of the song we continued our bizarre, "keep away from teacher," waltz.

I didn't know which was worse, Ms. Treble chasing me with a baton or the whole class staring at me. Suddenly the music stopped and my pants quit dancing.

Ms. Treble glared at me from across her desk.

"What is the meaning of this?" she demanded.

I had to think quick, so I said, "Ms. Treble, your music makes my pants want to get up and dance." Then I took a bow and ran out of the room.

As I passed Audrey, I noticed she was smiling. For the second time today, Audrey smiled at me!

Back in the hallway, to my amazement, I heard the sound of applause from Ms. Treble's room.

"You know pants, maybe you're not so bad after all. In fact, having you around might even be helpful in gym class."

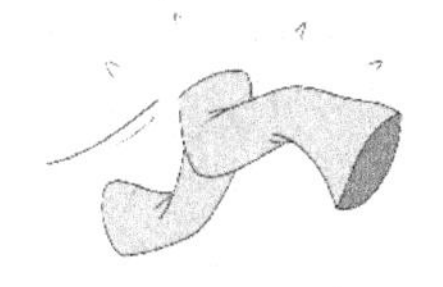

6

Don’t Mess Around With Gym

“I don’t do gym class,” said my pants.

“What do you mean ‘you don’t do gym class’?” I asked. “The second bell is about to ring and we’ll be in big trouble with Mr. Crunch if we’re late!”

“I’m sorry, but I don’t do gym,” said my pants. “I don’t need exercise to keep my shape. Besides, I hate when your legs get all sweaty. It gets gross down here.”

Just then the second bell rang for gym class. But my pants walked me right past the gym door!

Paul saw me and came running out after me.

“Hey, where are you going? We’ve got gym class now.”

“I know,” I said. I tried to turn back to face Paul as my pants walked me away. “But my pants have other ideas. It’s been a really weird morn-”

Bam!

I walked right into Rhino.

"That's it snotface! Third strike – you lose."

"Don't you mean, 'Third strike you're out'?" I asked.

"That's right," said Rhino. "You lose 'cause I'm gonna knock you out."

Me and my big mouth!

I turned to run back into the gym. I was thankful

that my pants weren't still fighting me. I could hear Rhino yelling, "Come back here twerp!" I was running as fast as I could to keep away from him. Everyone in gym class was watching me. I wasn't sure what to do.

Suddenly my pants said, "Lie down!"

"What?" I asked. "Are you crazy? If I lie down, Rhino will pulverize me!"

"No, he won't," said my pants. "Just trust me."

"No way!"

"Look out!" yelled Paul. "He's gaining on you!"

I made a sharp right turn and Rhino ran past me. His fingers grazed my shirt.

I ran back toward the door. But some of my classmates were standing in front of the exit, blocking it.

"Lie down now!" ordered my pants.

Since I was running out of options and running out of breath, I decided to give in and listen to my pants. I dove down and laid right there on the gym floor. I held my math notebook up to try to shield me from his punches.

The entire gym class closed in to witness the carnage as Rhino walked over to me.

"Now you die, twerp!"

He raised his fist and bent down to hit me. But before he could, there was a loud, "Riiiiippppp!"

His pants split wide open in the back!

The class laughed and pointed at Rhino's pants.

Rhino's face turned bright red. He turned around in circles, not sure who to direct his anger at as he surveyed the crowd of laughing faces.

Suddenly, he turned and bolted out the door.

The entire gym class started chanting, "Tyler! Tyler! Tyler!"

"How did you know he was going to split his pants?" I whispered to my pants.

"I know a thing or two about pants," he said. "But it really doesn't take a smarty pants to know you can't put a twenty pound turkey in a ten pound bag without something giving way."

Just as I was getting back on my feet, Mr. Crunch came in.

"What's going on?" he bellowed. "A kid running away in tears…People chanting someone's name... Has there been a fight in here? Tyler, did you beat up that poor little kid?"

"Little?" I thought to myself. "He's twice my size." But before I could say anything out loud, my pants were on the move again.

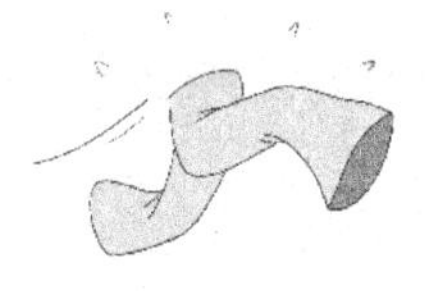

7

A Run in my Pants

"Just keep moving!" ordered my pants, as they took off for the door.

"Hey! Come back here Tyler!" yelled Mr. Crunch.

Just great. I barely managed to avoid getting mangled by someone twice my size, now I was being chased by someone twice *that* size. Before I knew what was happening, I was headed right for the back exit of the gym toward the playground.

"Come back here this minute!" yelled Mr. Crunch.

My pants and I kept moving. I hit the bump bar on the big door and sprinted to the playground. I ran as fast as I could and hid behind the climbing wall. This was more running than I would've done if I had just gone to gym class in the first place. This was probably more running than I had ever done in my life! I was breathing hard and heavy. I hoped Mr. Crunch wouldn't hear me.

Suddenly I heard a, "Hee Hee Hee!" coming from my pants.

"What's so funny," I whispered angrily. "Don't you know I'm about to get pulverized *and* sent to detention?"

"I'm sorry," said my pants. "It's just that I can't help noticing the irony. I'm the pants, but you're the one panting!"

"That's not funny!" I yelled.

"Ah ha!" yelled Mr. Crunch. "Now I've got you!"

He came running around the climbing wall. My pants and I took off in the opposite direction. We ran back into the gym.

"Let's get a leg up on him!" said my pants. Suddenly I found myself running up onto the bleachers!

But Mr. Crunch came racing right behind us! We were running out of bleachers! We had no choice but to make a jump for it. Now I was really flying by the seat of my pants!

Mr. Crunch jumped off after us. He was gaining on us!

"Drop your math notebook!" ordered my pants.

"But I need it to study for my test!" I yelled.

"You won't be able to take that test if he catches you!" replied my pants.

"OK," I said as I dropped my notebook behind me.

Mr. Crunch was so close behind me, he didn't have time to avoid the notebook. He slipped on the pages and fell into a long division!

I was able to make it to the door. I ducked out of the gym and ran down the hall.

"Now where do we go?" I asked.

I was looking to see if there were any vacant classrooms to hide in. I was thinking about locking myself in the janitor's closet for the rest of the day, when I saw that the door to the drama class was open. I rushed inside and shut the door. I looked back and didn't see any sign of Mr. Crunch.

I let out a deep breath of relief. I was ready for a break from all this drama.

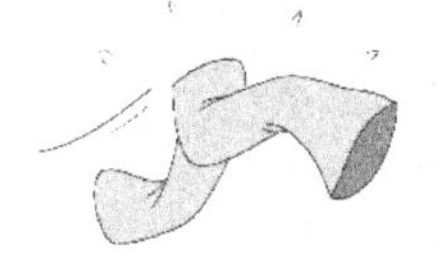

8

More Drama

"Are you here for the drama club talent show tryouts?" a voice behind me asked.

I turned around to see Ms. Catharsis, the drama teacher. I couldn't tell her the real reason I was in her class. But I didn't want to go back out in the hall and risk running into Mr. Crunch. So I said, "Yes I am."

"Excellent!" said Ms. Catharsis. "What is your talent?"

"My talent. Uh, my talent is..." I looked around the room hoping to find inspiration. I saw those weird smiley and frowny drama masks that always freak me out. I saw a bust of Shakespeare wearing one of those red, white and blue novelty wigs. I saw a rack of costume clothing. I saw…

"Yes," said Ms. Catharsis. "Your talent is?"

Suddenly I saw a box of puppets on a table.

"Ventriloquism," I answered, not quite believing myself as I said it.

"Wonderful!" said Ms. Catharsis. "Do you have your dummy with you? Or would you like to borrow one of our puppets for today?"

"I've got *my* dummy with me," said my pants.

I turned red and bit my lip as I tried to think of a way to hit my pants without hurting myself or looking like a total doofus.

"Wow, that was really good!" said Ms. Catharsis. "I didn't even see you move your lips. Why don't you go in the green room and get ready? You can go on right after Audrey sings her song."

Audrey? I couldn't believe I was going to get to see her again! Of course, there was also the chance that she would get to see me making a fool of myself again. I waited for Ms. Catharsis to take her attention off me. When she turned to the stage, I walked past the table and quickly grabbed a puppet from the box without looking.

I went to the green room, which was really just a part of the class separated by a big, green curtain. It was right next to the "stage," which was just another part of the room that was taped off with masking tape. I peeked out to make sure no one was nearby. Then I explained my plan to my pants.

"I need you to do the voice of this… donkey." I said, finally looking at the puppet I grabbed.

"You know, you really don't have to explain this to me. I *am* a smarty pants."

"I know, I know. Just try not to get me in trouble this time, OK?"

My pants said something in response, but I hardly noticed. Audrey had begun singing. Her voice was as pretty as the rest of her! I watched from the green room on the side of the stage as she sang the most beautiful version of "America the Beautiful" that I had ever heard. When she finished, I clapped wildly from the side of the stage.

Audrey looked over, surprised to see someone on the side of the stage. When she saw that it was me, she smiled. Then she turned and said, "Thank you," to whatever Ms. Catharsis just said to her.

I was still thinking about Audrey's smile when I heard Ms. Catharsis call out, "All right Tyler, you're next!"

I walked on stage, with the donkey puppet on my left hand. I saw Ms. Catharsis in the front row. I also saw Audrey lingering by the door. My throat went dry and my mind went blank. I stood there like a statue with no idea what to do.

Suddenly I heard my pants say, "Say something, dummy."

“Stop calling me a dummy!” I yelled before I could even think.

Ms. Catharsis laughed.

Audrey laughed too!

I suddenly remembered what I had gotten myself into. When I heard my pants talk again, I tried to move the donkey’s mouth in sync.

“Then stop acting like a dummy!” said my pants as I moved my donkey’s mouth.

"I guess I've been hanging around you too long," I said. "You're starting to rub off on me."

"Rub off on you? I'd be happy to *get* off of you!"

"Why don't you go ahead then? But I bet you won't get too far without me!"

"And I bet you'd look pretty naked without me!"

Back and forth, my pants and I argued. It felt good to finally let out a day's worth of frustration, without anybody knowing I was some kind of nut job who has heated arguments with his pants. Before I knew it, the bell rang.

Ms. Catharsis stood up and clapped.

"Wonderful!" she said. "You're in! I can't wait to see what you come up with for next month's show!"

Next month's show? I didn't think I'd actually make the cut. What was I going to do now?

Before I could think about how to weasel out of it, Audrey walked up and said, "That was pretty cool! I'll see you in math class."

Cool! She said I was cool!

Math class? I forgot about math class!

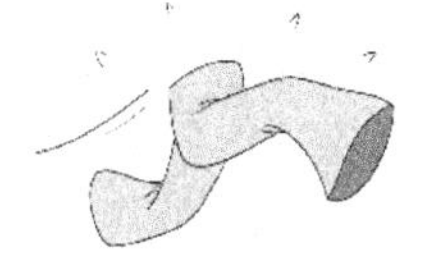

9

Adding It Up

I rushed out of the drama classroom and nearly knocked down Paul.

"Hey kid, watch where… Oh, it's you!" said Paul. "I've been looking all over for you. Because of you, we didn't have gym class today. Apparently, Mr. Crunch pulled a muscle chasing after you, so we got a free period – you're the school hero!"

"Hero?" I repeated. "That's a new one. Too bad it won't do me any good when Rhino finds me - or when my parents find out I failed my math test."

"What are you worried about?" asked Paul. "Just use your talking pants like I said earlier."

"I do *not* help people cheat!" cried my pants.

"Verbal encouragement!" countered Paul.

"We can't have this conversation here." I said. "Let's find somewhere private."

So Paul and I went into the boy's restroom by the gym. We had to wait for a couple of first graders to leave before we could talk. By the time they finished, the second bell rang.

"What's going on?" asked Paul. "It's not like you to be late for class like this."

"It's my pants!" I said. "He's not just talking, he's controlling where my legs take me!"

"He?" asked Paul. "If it's a pair of pants, shouldn't it be 'they'?"

"I don't know!" I yelled. "I'm not sure that's the most important thing right now. How can I get them to stop driving me crazy?"

"Crazy?" cried my pants. "Crazy! All I did today was get your crush Audrey to notice you, save you from a bully, and make you a school hero for cancelling gym class!"

"That's true," I admitted. "But you also got me in trouble with Rhino in the first place. Plus, I'm going to have detention because of your little running man show in gym. AND I'm probably going to fail this math test because you wouldn't give me a minute of peace all day to study."

"I'm confused," said Paul. "Are you happy with the pants or not?"

"I don't know," I confessed. "All I know is that good or bad, these pants are stressing me out! I don't think I can handle this kind of constant drama all day long."

"So just tell your pants to button his lip for the rest of the day," said Paul.

"Hey nobody talks to me like that!" said my pants. "Nobody hems me in!"

"I'll talk to you however I want," said Paul. "You're just a dumb pair of pants."

"I'm a *smart* pair of pants," argued my pants. "I'm way smarter than you. I bet even your dumb pants are smarter than you."

"You better stop, right now!" said Paul.

"I'd like to see you make me," said my pants.

"Don't make me belt you!" shouted Paul.

"That's it!" I cried. "Paul, take off your belt. I'll be right back."

I ran out to my locker and got my sport bag with my soccer gear. I went back to the restroom and borrowed Paul's belt. I took off my pants. He resisted as hard as he could, flailing around like one of those inflatable balloon men at the used car lots.

"Don't take me off!" cried my pants. "I'll be good, I promise! I don't want to be alone!"

I finally managed to get my pants off. I balled them up and tied them in place with Paul's belt. As I stuffed him in my sport bag, I could still hear his muffled cries.

"Don't put me in here! It's dark in here! Somebody turn on a light!"

"I've got to say," said Paul. "That is the weirdest thing I have ever witnessed."

I put on my soccer shorts and stood up.

"It was even weirder from this end!" I replied.

"Now what?" asked Paul.

"Now we go to math," I said.

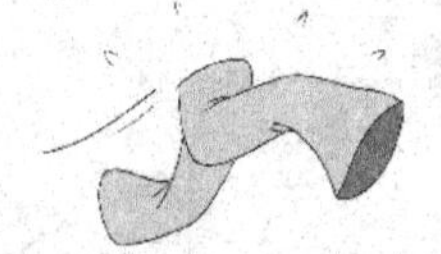

10

Math Problem

"So nice of you two to join us," said Mr. Hypotenuse when we walked into math class. "I'm so sorry my class is interfering with your schedule. Would you be so kind as to tell us why you're honoring us with your presence ten minutes *after* the start of class?"

I could never understand Mr. Hypotenuse when he was talking numbers. When he used words, it was even harder. I think he was asking us why we were late. Paul looked at me and shrugged like he wanted me to say something.

"Well," I began. "It's kind of a long story, and I feel bad for being late. So, I really shouldn't take up any more of your time."

"Sometimes," said Mr. Hypotenuse, "the shortest distance between two points is the truth."

"You want me to tell you the truth?" I asked.

"If it's not too much trouble," he replied.

I looked at Mr. Hypotenuse. I looked at the class. I knew no one would believe the truth. But I had to come up with something.

"Paul and I had to save a, um…"

"Baby bird!" interrupted Paul.

"And what kind of bird was it," asked Mr. Hypotenuse.

"A robin," I said.

"An eagle," said Paul at the same time.

‘Robin-Eagles are very rare,” said Mr. Hypotenuse. “Apparently, so is honesty. Why don’t you try telling me the truth this time?”

I looked at the class. It felt like a thousand eyes were watching me. I knew I would never be able to live this down, but I was out of options.

So I explained the whole ordeal of my talking pants and Rhino and gym class. (I left out the parts about Audrey ‘cause that was kind of personal.) But I did tell him that I really tried to study but my pants wouldn’t let me.

“And that’s why I should be excused from taking this test today,” I explained. “And that’s also why I’m wearing my soccer shorts.”

The whole class busted out laughing.

So much for being the school hero. I was back to being Tyler the twerp.

Mr. Hypotenuse put his hand on his forehead and looked down at the floor. “Tyler, lies don’t sit well with me. I suggest you and Paul sit down and get ready for your test. We’ll talk about your tardiness after class.”

I took my seat and prepared for the worst.

But it got worse.

Sarah volunteered to pass out the tests. She stuck her tongue out as she handed one to me.

I looked at the first problem and tried to concentrate. But I kept thinking about my weird day. I hated to admit it, but my pants really did make things more exciting. I went back to my problem. Then I started thinking about Audrey and the way she smiled at me.

"All right class," said Mr. Hypotenuse. "You have five more minutes to finish your tests."

Uuuggggg! Only five minutes!

I whipped through the questions as fast as I could. Some of the stuff looked familiar, but I didn't have time to double check any answers. I was still working on the last problem when I heard Mr. Hypotenuse say, "Pencils down!"

I knew I bombed the test. But that wasn't even the worst part.

Mr. Hypotenuse likes to give us worksheets after a test so he can grade the tests and announce our grades right away. He always says he does that to reward our efforts. But we all knew he does it to embarrass the kids who didn't study.

Now I was one of those kids!

As we did our worksheets, Mr. Hypotenuse called out grades as he finished checking our tests.

"Simone, you earned a B+"

"Earned," that was another of his tricks.

Everyone knew he didn't use that word to praise the kids who got A's, he used it to embarrass the ones who got bad grades. Like someone would be proud to "earn" a D!

"Sarah, congratulations. You earned an A+"

"I can't stand that little smarty pants!" whispered Paul from the seat behind me.

Mr. Hypotenuse kept grading as we fumbled with our worksheets. I was watching the clock, hoping for the bell before he got to my test.

"Tyler,"

Oh no, here it comes.

"You, and your magical pants, earned a C-"

Everyone laughed. I wasn't sure which was worse, hearing everyone laugh at me again or having to tell my parents I got a lousy C- on my test.

"Paul, you earned a C- as well."

"All right!" cheered Paul. "That's my best grade so far!"

Just then the bell rang. I got up and bolted for the door.

"Not so fast, Tyler!" called Mr. Hypotenuse. "You too Paul. We still need to discuss your, 'grand entrance,' to class today."

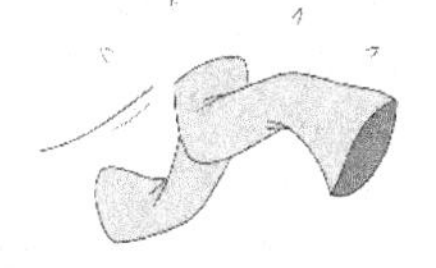

11
After Math

So here I am, cleaning the boards, straightening chairs, and picking up trash for Mr. Hypotenuse.

Paul had just run out for a quick restroom break when who should walk by, but Rhino – in a pair of soccer shorts!

"You!" he grunted. "I've got something…"

He stopped and looked at me funny.

"Hey, why are you wearing soccer shorts too?" he asked. "Are you trying to make fun of me?"

Uh oh. This was not good. At least in the gym there was a crowd who could step in if things got too bad. Now I had to face him all alone.

I looked at him and tried to figure out what to say. For a second, I wished I had my crazy talking pants back.

But as I looked at Rhino, he didn't seem as big as he did this morning. He almost looked like a normal kid. So I decided to just talk to him like a normal kid.

"No, I'm not making fun of you," I said. "I know what it feels like to have a whole class laugh at you. I put on my soccer shorts so you wouldn't be the only kid in school wearing them."

Rhino stared at me like he was trying to decide which part of me to break first. Then he walked toward me and swung his right hand forward – for me to shake!

"That's the nicest thing anyone's ever done for me," he said. "What's your name kid?"

"Tyler," I answered.

"Well, Tyler," said Rhino, "from now on I got your back. If anyone ever gives you any trouble, you just let me know. OK?"

"Yeah, OK," I said. "If there's anything I can do for you, you let me know too."

Rhino laughed and punched me in the arm. "That's a good one, Tyler! If I ever need help, you'll be the first person I call! Now let's get out of here, it smells like learning in here."

I laughed and tried to resist rubbing my arm where he punched me.

We walked out the door and ran into Paul.

"Hey Ty…" he stopped short.

"Is everything OK?" he asked, moving his eyes back and forth between me and Rhino.

"Everything's fine," I said. "Rob and I were just getting ready to catch the bus. Why don't you come with us?"

So Rob, Paul and I got our stuff from our lockers and headed for the busses.

Suddenly we heard a voice coming from my sport bag.

"Hey, let me out! It smells like dirty socks in here!"

"Who said that?" asked Rob.

"That was uh, that was me," I said. "I'm working on a ventriloquist act for the talent show next month."

"Hmmmm," said Rob. "Maybe you *will* come in handy one day. Well, there's my bus. I'll see you around!"

As we walked to our bus, Paul asked, "How did you keep Rhino from beating you to a pulp?"

"I'm not sure," I answered. "But it's weird. Every time I tell the truth, no one believes me. And every time I lie, people think I'm telling the truth."

"That *is* weird," said Paul. "But it could be worse. You could be like me and have nobody believe you no matter what you say. At least people believe you half the time."

"Yeah, I guess you're right." I said.

"For what it's worth," said Paul. "I believe you."

"Thanks Paul. I'm not sure I would believe everything that happened today if I didn't have you for a witness."

"What do you think caused it?" asked Paul.

"I have no idea," I said. "Maybe mom used some weird new detergent. Maybe it was a passing comet. Maybe someone was using mind control…"

"Well, at least it's over," said Paul. "It's not like anything that weird could happen again."

"You got that right!" yelled my pants from inside the bag. "From now on I'm keeping my lip buttoned up! First chance I get, I'm going to split! You won't have me to kick around in anymore! ..."

I dropped the sport bag on the sidewalk to see if that would stop him from talking. He went quiet.

"I hope not," I said to Paul. "I don't think I could handle another weird day like--"

Just then I saw Audrey wave to me as her bus drove by.

"Then again, maybe I could."

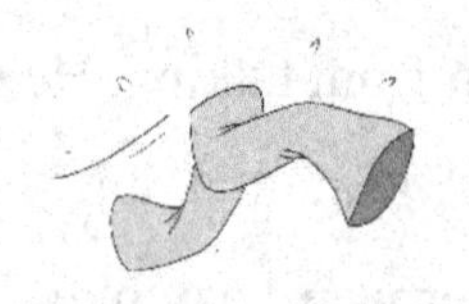

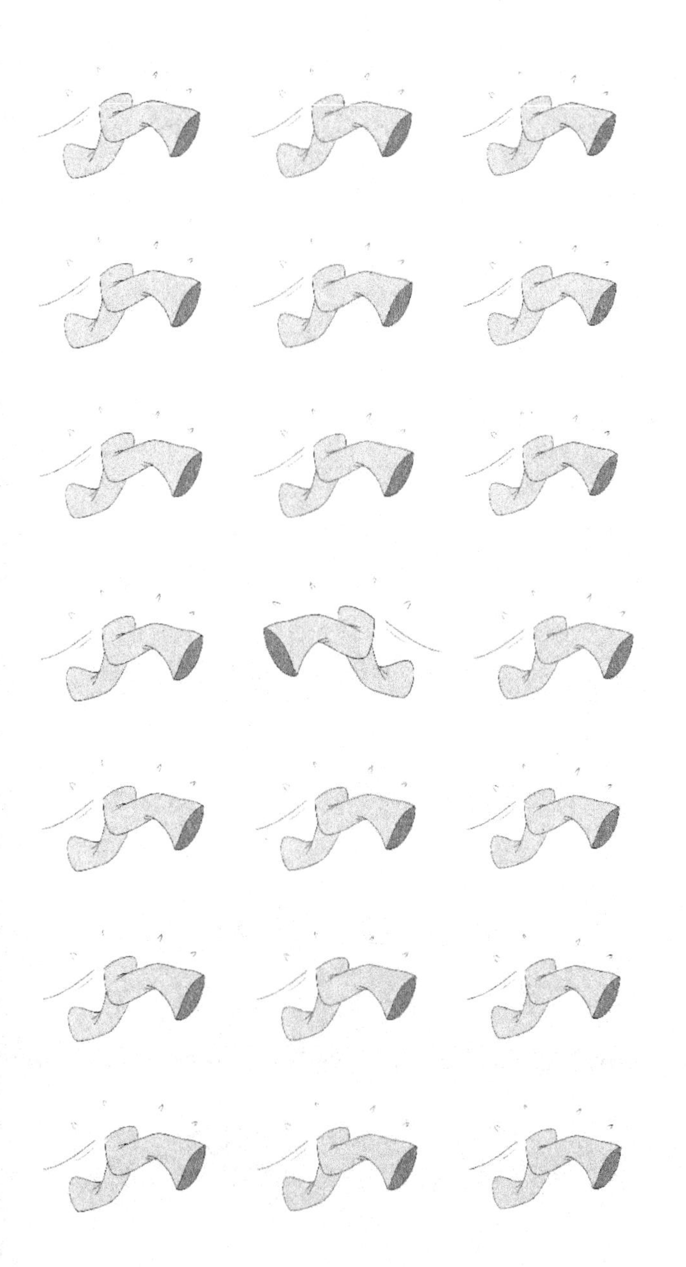

Tyler will return in Tyler File #2…

Hollow Weenie!

"Did you notice anything else unusual?" I asked. "Like maybe a moldy hot dog that moved on its own?"

"You mean like that?" said Paul, pointing to the cafeteria door.

It was my hot dog! It had grown five times its original size!

It ran into the cafeteria and yelled, "FEED ME!"

Everyone freaked out and ran to the back of the room!

We all stood and watched as the hot dog ate our lunches.

Paul cried out, "Hey, your homework ate my dog!"

"*Your* homework?" said Sarah. "I might have known you had something to do with this Tyler! ..."

Talking With Tyler

Wow! That was one weird day! I can't believe my own pants started talking! (and talking, and talking…)

What do you think could have caused it?

What is the weirdest thing you've ever experienced?

Did you tell anyone about it? Did they believe you?

I'm lucky to have my friend Paul. I can trust him with my secrets. Who is the one person in the world you could trust with *anything*?

My talking and leg-controlling pants were crazy embarrassing. What's the most embarrassing thing that's ever happened to you?

How many people saw it happen? Who were they? Did they laugh? How did it make you feel?

Did anyone cheer you up after it happened? Who? How?

I really like Audrey, but I'm not sure how to let her know. Have you ever had a secret crush? Did she/he ever find out?

I think Rob might actually be a nice kid, once I get to know him. Have you ever changed your mind about a person? Who was it? What made you change your mind?

What If?

Having my pants come to life was certainly the weirdest thing that's ever happened to me. But I suppose there were some good parts to it. They did help me get Audrey's attention. And they did save me from Rob.

What if you could choose one everyday object and make it come to life…

What object would you bring to life? Why?

What do you think it would say?

What do you think it would do?

How could it potentially make your life better?

How could it make your life worse?

How would it affect others?

Who would you share it with?

Who would you hide it from?

How would you stop it if it got out of control?!?!

What's So Funny About Pants?

There's nothing funny about leg-controlling, bossy, talking pants. But sometimes you just have to laugh at what life brings. So, here are my favorite jokes about pants.

Why doesn't Piglet's best friend wear pants?

He doesn't want to get Pooh on them!

Why did the pants think his tailor was funny?

He always left him in stitches!

What song do pants love the most?

Zipper-de-do-da!

What books do pants like best?

Pocket books!

What happens when your mom's sisters go shopping for new jeans?

They get aunts in their pants!

What do you call pants for dogs?

Bowser trousers!

What do mean girls wear at Halloween?

Witches' britches!

Why do firemen wear red suspenders?

To hold up their pants!

Why do firemen wear red belts?

In case the suspenders break!

What superhero do pants fear most?

Iron Man!

What dessert do pants like least?

Banana *splits*!

What sci-fi movie do pants like best?

The Fly!

10 Fun Facts About Pants

Here are 10 things my smarty pants wants everyone to know about pants.

1 The first ever jeans were invented by Levi Strauss for California gold miners who wanted a tough material for their "britches" that wouldn't fall apart after a hard day of mining.

2 The first pair of Levi's cost $1.25.

3 Jeans are made from a sturdy cotton weave fabric called serge that comes from Nimes (pronounced nim), France. The "serge de Nimes" was later shorted to "denim" in America.

4 Blue jeans were once banned at many schools, churches and restaurants because they were considered "rebellious."

5 On average, every American owns 7 pairs of jeans.

6 Technically, “khaki” is not a type of pants, it is a color.

7 The word “Khaki” comes from the Hindi word for “Dusty.”

8 In ancient China, pants were called “chinos” and were only worn by soldiers.

9 In England, the word “pants” usually refers to underwear.

10 Being a “liar, liar” will not actually cause your pants to catch fire.

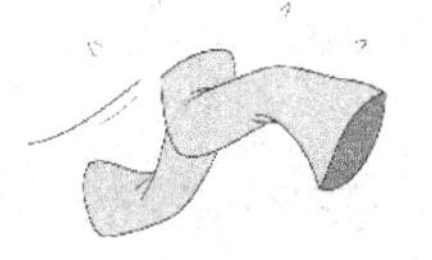

When are pants not pants?

When they're an idiom!

An idiom is a phrase that has a meaning different from its literal meaning. (A famous example of an idiom is, "It's raining cats and dogs.")

Here are my ten favorite pants idioms:

1. **Ants in the pants**

(to be nervous and agitated)

I have ants in my pants whenever Audrey is around!

2. **Smarty pants**

(someone who thinks they're smarter than everyone else)

That Sarah is such a smarty pants!

3. **Fancy pants**

(trying to appear more attractive or clever than you really are)

I hate being a fancy pants on school picture day!

4. A kick in the pants

(a strong message or demand; or an unpleasant event)

Mr. Hypotenuse's tests are always a kick in the pants!

5. Wear the pants in the family

(to be in charge)

My mom wears the pants in our family!

6. Flying by the seat of your pants

(doing something difficult without proper training)

The first day of soccer practice, I was really flying by the seat of my pants!

7. Scare the pants off

(to frighten someone intensely)

Paul scared the pants off me last Halloween!

8. Caught with your pants down

(to be caught in the act of doing something wrong)

Paul got caught with his pants down when he toilet-papered the neighbor's house last year!

9. Put on your big boy pants

(to be brave or mature)

I had to put on my big boy pants to face Rob alone!

10. Keep your pants on

(to be patient)

Keep your pants on, I'll have another story soon!

Thanks so much for reading about my adventures! If you enjoyed the story, please ask your parents to leave a review wherever they bought the book; and tell your friends about the book to help spread the word about THE TYLER FILES!

Don't forget to check out Tyler File #2
Hollow Weenie!

Be sure to visit
www.BrianRock.net
to keep up with Tyler's latest adventures!

Parents can email the word "Howdy" to
BrianRock@brianrock.us to sign up for his newsletter.

Other Books by Brian Rock

Chapter Books

THE TYLER FILES

#1 Smarty Pants!

#2 Hollow Weenies!

#3 My Nose Is Running!

Picture Books

MARTIAN MUSTACHE MISCHIEF

DON'T PLAY WITH YOUR FOOD!

THE DEDUCTIVE DETECTIVE

WITH ALL MY HEART

PIGGIES

About the author:

Brian Rock is a children's author and former school teacher who lives in Chesterfield, VA with his wife, daughter, Aussie-doodle and, of course, his many imaginary friends.

Brian's pants have never actually talked to him; and any sounds coming from his pants are certainly not his fault!

CPSIA information can be obtained
at www.ICGtesting.com
Printed in the USA
FSOW03n0652131217
42371FS